KT-513-240

A Knit and a Knot

'A Knit and a Knot'
An original concept by Amanda Brandon
© Amanda Brandon

Illustrated by Catalina Echeverri

Published by MAVERICK ARTS PUBLISHING LTD

Studio 3A, City Business Centre, 6 Brighton Road,

Horsham, West Sussex, RH13 5BB

© Maverick Arts Publishing Limited November 2018

+44 (0)1403 256941

A CIP catalogue record for this book is available at the British Library.

ISBN 978-1-84886-387-3

Maverick
publishing
www.maverickbooks.co.uk

Orange

This book is rated as: Orange Band (Guided Reading)
The original picture book text for this story has been
modified by the author to be an early reader.

A Knit and a Knot

by Amanda Brandon

illustrated by
Catalina Echeverri

Granny Mutton was teaching

Lionel to knit.

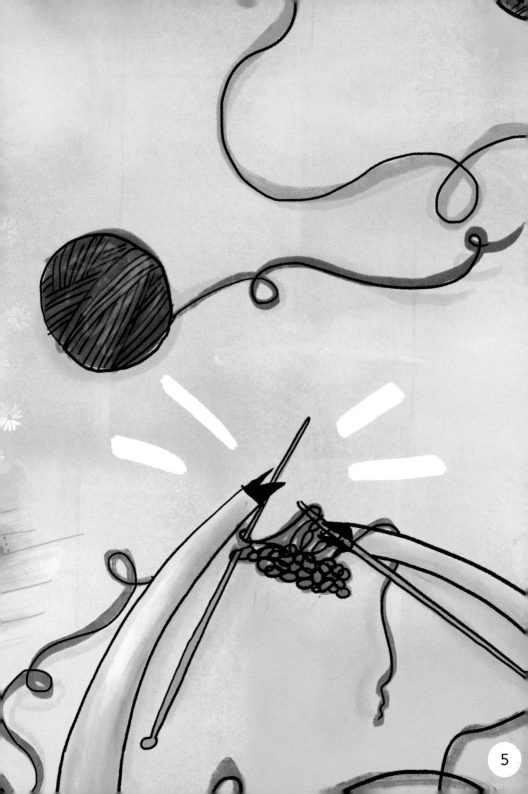

He was knitting squares but it wasn't easy.

"This is more like knotting than knitting,"

he said.

"You're doing well," Granny said.

"You can use my new red wool.

That's easy to knit with."

They looked high and they looked low
but they couldn't find it.

"My lovely new wool has gone," Granny said.

"Don't worry, I'll find it," Lionel said.

He set off from Granny's house.

Soon he saw Rocky the sheep-dog.

"Granny has lost her wool," said Lionel.

"Can you help?"

"Look! There's some red wool
on the bush," Rocky said.

Lionel tried to grab the wool but it suddenly whipped away.

He fell in the hedge. "Ouch!"

"Someone pulled that wool away from me."

"There must be a wool thief in the farmyard."

"Let's run after them!" Rocky said.

But then they heard a rumble

behind them.

It was a big bull.

"This means trouble," Lionel shouted.

They jumped over the fence.

SPLASH!

Into the duck pond.

"Now we've lost the trail," Lionel said.

"Not yet." Rocky pointed to some little footprints. They followed the footprints to the barn.

Lionel saw some wool caught on the door.

They had found the thief.

They pulled the wool...

Someone tugged the other end.

They pulled again.

The wool whizzed over their heads.

"HELP!"

The thief shouted as he dropped
into a big pile of straw.

Rocky and Lionel
went to the rescue.

"Pipsqueak!" they said in surprise.

"Why did you take Granny's wool?"

"I'm sorry," Pipsqueak said.

"I wanted wool to make a bed for

my new brothers and sisters."

"You have to give it back," Lionel said.

"But I've got something you

can have instead."

He fetched his knitting and sang,

"Make a square with a knit and a knot

to make the perfect mouse's cot."

And he tucked a mouse

under each square.

Pipsqueak, Rocky and Lionel returned the wool to Granny Mutton.

"Thank you, you're just in time,"

she said.

Quiz

1. What is Granny Mutton teaching Lionel in the beginning?
a) How to sing
b) How to make toast
c) How to knit

2. Who does Lionel meet when he leaves Granny's house?
a) Rocky
b) Scotty
c) Ratty

3. But then they heard a rumble behind them. It was a big _____?
a) Chicken
b) Bull
c) Tiger

4. What kind of animal is the wool thief?

a) Dog
b) Sheep
c) Mouse

5. Why did Pipsqueak take the wool?
a) He is starting a knitting club
b) He wanted to make a bed
c) For fun

Book Bands for Guided Reading

The Institute of Education book banding system is a scale of colours that reflects the various levels of reading difficulty. The bands are assigned by taking into account the content, the language style, the layout and phonics. Word, phrase and sentence level work is also taken into consideration.

Maverick Early Readers are a bright, attractive range of books covering the pink to white bands. All of these books have been book banded for guided reading to the industry standard and edited by a leading educational consultant.

To view the whole Maverick Readers scheme, visit our website at

www.maverickearlyreaders.com

Or scan the QR code above to view our scheme instantly!

Quiz Answers: 1c, 2a, 3b, 4c, 5b